Grover, Messenger of Love

A Random House PICTUREBACK®

Random House/Children's Television Workshop

Library of Congress Cataloging-in-Publication Data
Thackray, Patricia. Grover, messenger of love / by Patricia Thackray ; illustrated by Joe Ewers. p. cm. — (A Random House pictureback) "Featuring Jim Henson's Sesame Street Muppets." SUMMARY: Grover serves as a messenger of love for a prince and princess separated by a garden wall. ISBN 0-679-87863-7 [1. Walls—Fiction. 2. Princes—Fiction. 3. Princesses—Fiction. 4. Puppets—Fiction.] I. Ewers, Joe, ill. II. Title. PZ7.T298Gr 1996 [E]—dc20 95-18799
Manufactured in the United States of America 10 9 8 7 6 5 4 3 2 1

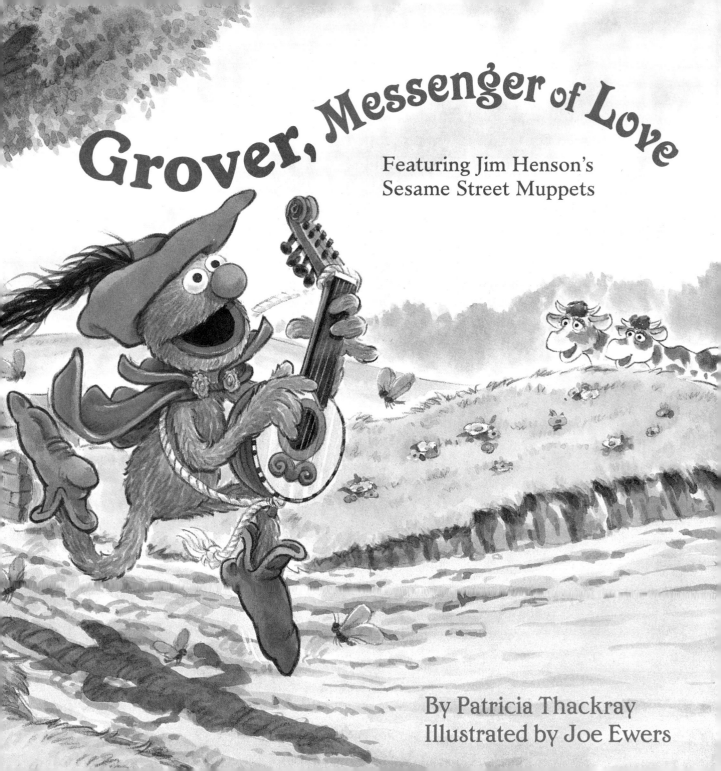

Grover, Messenger of Love

Featuring Jim Henson's
Sesame Street Muppets

By Patricia Thackray
Illustrated by Joe Ewers

One day Grover was skipping along, strumming his lute, when he heard the sound of someone crying. It was a beautiful princess weeping by her garden wall.

"Do not cry, beautiful princess. I, Grover, will play you a happy tune on my cute little lute," he said.

"It won't help," wailed the princess. "I am crying because of this stupid wall."

"But it looks like such a nice wall," said Grover.

"It is a *horrible* wall," said the princess. "I am the lovely Lucretia. My next-door neighbor and true love, Lorenzo, lives on the other side. We used to play together all the time. But one day my father's pet goat, Lulu, ate up Lorenzo's father's red woolly underwear that was hanging out to dry. Lorenzo's father was so angry that he built this awful wall. And from that day on, Lorenzo and I have been apart."

"What a sad story," said Grover, beginning to sniffle.

"Wait. It gets even sadder," said Lucretia. "I wrote this love letter for Lorenzo and sprinkled it with my best perfume. But he will never read it."

"Why not?" asked Grover. "You mean he cannot read yet?"

"Oh, he can read," said Lucretia. "But I can't get the letter to him because of this stupid wall."

"Say no more, fair princess," said Grover. He took the letter from Lucretia. "I, Grover, will be your Messenger of Love."

Grover took off his hat and bowed very low. Just then, Lulu the goat charged up behind him and butted him over the wall.

"Airmail special-delivery love letter!" yelled Grover.

Grover landed smack on top of the handsome Lorenzo.

"*Oof!* Where did *you* come from?" cried Lorenzo.

"From the other side of your father's wall. I have a love letter from the fair Lucretia," said Grover.

Lorenzo read the letter. He almost fainted from happiness and too much perfume.

"Good fellow, please take this to the lovely Lucretia," said
Lorenzo, handing Grover an enormous chest full of precious jewels.
"This is very heavy," gasped Grover. He sat down on one end
of Lorenzo's silver seesaw. "How will I ever get it over the wall?"

The handsome Lorenzo, who was also quite smart, had an idea.
"Get ready, furry Messenger of Love!" he shouted. Then he
climbed onto a chair and jumped on the other end of the seesaw.
"Here I go again!" cried Grover as he flew over the wall.

"Oh, Messenger of Love!" said Lucretia. "Do you bring a message from Lorenzo?"

"I do have a little something for you," croaked Grover.

"Wow! Jewels!" exclaimed the fair Lucretia. "Just what I needed."

Then she reached behind a rosebush and pulled out a life-size portrait of herself.

"You must take this to my love," she said.

"I am going over the wall *again?*" said Grover "Being a Messenger of Love is a lot of hard work!"

He sat down in Lucretia's velvet swing. "Please excuse me for a minute while I take a little nap."

"This is no time for a rest," said Lucretia. She gave the swing a big push, and Grover flew over the wall once more.

Grover's head crashed through the portrait as he landed at Lorenzo's feet.

"It is I, Grover, in a beautiful portrait of your love," he said, smiling bravely up at Lorenzo.

Lorenzo handed Grover a big silver tray piled high with steaming tarts. "Here, Grover. While you were away I baked Lucretia's favorite treat—Tickleberry Tarts."

Lorenzo helped Grover onto his silken trampoline.
"Hurry, Grover, before they get cold," said Lorenzo.
"One…two…*threeeeeeee!*" sang Grover. "Here comes your
tired, furry Messenger of Love!"

Grover flew over the wall again and landed with a splash in Lucretia's goldfish pond.

"The tarts!" cried Grover. "I must save them!"

He balanced the tray on his cute little tummy and backstroked to shore.

"Oh, joy! My favorite treat—Tickleberry Tarts!" said Lucretia. "Grover, you must take another gift to Lorenzo for me. I have just the thing."

"I am *so* cold and *so* tired," sighed Grover. "But I, Grover, Messenger of Love, cannot disappoint such adorable lovers."

Lucretia held up a suit of armor.

"Lorenzo will look so romantic in this!" she sighed.

"Maybe you could just blow him a kiss instead?" asked Grover
hopefully.

"Don't be silly, Grover," said Lucretia, stuffing him into the armor.

"But it is so heavy," panted Grover. "How am I supposed to get it
over the wall?"

"Love will find a way," said Lucretia sweetly. "Come along now. Hop
onto my golden skateboard and I'll give you a push down this little hill."

Whooooosh! Grover whizzed down the hill.

"Don't forget to jump!" cried Lucretia.

Then…CLANG! The visor on Grover's helmet slammed shut. He couldn't see a thing.

"Jump, Grover! Jump!" cried the lovely Lucretia.

But it was too late. Grover smashed right through the wall.

Lucretia and Lorenzo found themselves staring
at each other through a big Grover-shaped hole.
"Lorenzo!" cried Lucretia.
"Lucretia!" cried Lorenzo.
"Mom-meee!" cried Grover.

"Thank you for bringing us together again, noble sir," said Lorenzo.

"It was nothing," gasped Grover, staggering over to Lucretia and Lorenzo. "Now that you are happy once more, it is time for me to bid you farewell and go home to my mommy and my nap."

"Wait! One last favor," said Lucretia. "On your way home, could you please deliver these invitations? We're having a party to celebrate."

"Oh my goodness!" cried Grover, Messenger of Love, and he fell over backward in a faint.